Bible Dramatizations, Book 1

A Collection of Short Stories

C. J. Korryn

Published by C. J. Korryn Books, 2019.

D0913629

Published by:

C. J. Korryn Books

****

©2019 by C. J. Korryn

****

Visit C. J. Korryn's website below for more of his
books.

http://authorcjkorryn.wixsite.com/officialwebsite/books

Table of Contents

The Adulteress

She was being dragged and pulled by Cairion, the head teacher of religious law, and a pharisee she did not recognize.

Blinking away blinding tears of despair, she more stumbled than walked. Barely able to see through tear-soaked eyes, she kept stepping on pebble after pebble and stick after stick. They dug into her feet, and the hot dirt burned her bare feet as she was dragged to her doom, a reminder of what awaited her minutes away.

Her wrist stung, and she could already feel the bruises forming where Cairion and the pharisee pulled at her. With her other hand, she held, wrapped about her, a bed sheet. The only thing between her shame and all of the eyes boring into her.

When they first came into her bedroom, she screamed pleas of mercy as they dragged her from her bed and pulled her out of her house and down her street for all of her neighbors to see.

She no longer pleaded, merely wept, her bruised cheek and bloodied lip a testament of the futility in trying to resist God's servants of righteousness.

"Teacher!" said Cairion. "Teacher!"

She felt a hand let go of her wrist, then she was flung so hard to the ground she slid several inches feeling the sheet wrapped around her rip at her knees, and the searing pain of hot sand grinding deep into her knees.

She caught herself with her free hand, adding another surge of pain. Her bruised wrist jarred to a stop, and the hot dirt burning into her palm.

"This woman was caught in the act of adultery. The law of Moses says to stone her. What do *you* say?" Cairion asked.

The woman wrapped the sheet tight around her, exposed, ashamed. She wanted nothing more than to run away. But run where? She couldn't run home; they would just go get her again. She couldn't run to the man she had been with; he was with them now, ready to stone her. She had no family, and she had no friends who would take her in now.

She stared at the dirt beneath her, her tears turning it to mud. She was too ashamed to look up, to see the condemning eyes of the crowd, the murderous stares of the pharisees, the judging gaze of the teacher.

She felt the heat of their eyes drilling into her and the burn of the sun seeping through the thin sheet.

She wrapped the sheet tighter again, a symbol of her shame. She held tight to it, the only comfort she had, a sanctuary that she wrapped around her as she stared deep into her puddle of tears.

The teacher did not answer, and Cairion and several of the pharisees demanded an answer.

A hush came over the crowd, and she still dared not to look up.

"Alright, stone her," the teacher answered.

The woman gasped in despair; she knew she was going to be stoned, but to hear it ordered out loud sent a wave of paralyzing fear through her she had never felt before. She began to shake, and she could barely breathe. Her body began to tingle where she imagined the first few stones would hit: the back of her head, her shoulder, her back, and even her face, all tingled in horrific anticipation of her death.

She heard her captors picking up the instruments of her death.

"But let the one who has never sinned throw the first stone," the woman heard the teacher say.

She closed her eyes, awaiting her death, already feeling where the first stones would contact.

She heard a thump so loud that she shook in fright.

Another thump.

Two more thumps.

Then another, and another, and another.

She slowly inched her head up, expecting a rock to the face, but what she saw astonished her. She gasped in shock and relief. One by one, the pharisees were walking away. The youngest—the one she had been with when they came—walked away from her, his eyes never even glancing toward her.

She wondered why it was only her there to be condemned and not him, as well. After all, he was guilty of the same sin.

"Woman," the teacher said as he stood. "Where are your accusers? Didn't even one of them condemn you?" he asked.

"No, Lord," she replied.

"Neither do I. Go and sin no more."

She stared at Jesus, immensely grateful that he did not condemn her. She stared at him several moments as he began speaking to the crowd again as he had been speaking to them when she had been brought before him.

She wrapped her sheet tight again but did not leave.

He had not condemned her, and he had kept the pharisees from condemning her. She wanted to learn more about Jesus, and she wanted to hear what he was saying to the crowd.

She saw Jesus look back at her as he began teaching, but not with eyes of disapproval as the crowd did but eyes that cared, accepting eyes.

She stayed until Jesus had finished speaking, and she couldn't help but feel like he had been speaking specifically to her the entire time.

She wrapped her sheet around her and smiled. She saw the torn fabric from where the pharisees had thrown her. A symbol of her brokenness healed; a manifestation of her sins taken away. She wrapped the sheet around her as tight as she could and smiled, her sheet no longer a symbol of shame but a covering of her grace.

The Sister of Lazarus

Mary and Martha held each other in grief as they walked behind Jesus. Their beloved brother's death four days earlier had brought a new measure of sorrow and despair that they had never known before.

They were thirty-seven years old and, yet, looked closer to their late forties as the past few days had taken a heavy toll on them. Their younger brother, Lazarus, had fallen ill a week before and died rather quickly.

A crowd followed the twins, wailing and weeping, which brought little comfort to the sisters as most of them did not know the family but were merely there to "mourn" with them.

Mary seemed to be taking her younger brother's death much harder than Martha. She mumbled regularly under her breath that he was only twenty-three. She couldn't understand why God would allow—why Jesus would let—him die at such a young age.

The Christ walked before her, and yet, He had chosen not to save her brother. But He was here now—too late, but still, He was here, and she knew He would do something.

They were nearing Lazarus' tomb now, and she heard the "mourners" behind her begin to mumble to each other as she and her sister clung to each other in sorrow.

She heard a voice behind her boldly ask his neighbor, "Could not He who opened the eyes of the blind man have kept this man from dying?"

The man's neighbor was about to reply but saw Mary snap her head around with an ice-cold glare. She was about to say something when Martha gently grabbed her check.

"Ignore them, Mary. Nothing they say matters," she said, glaring at the two herself. The two fell silent for the rest of the walk.

Mary didn't really know why she became so infuriated at the man's comment. Maybe it was because she wondered the same thing. Jesus had healed many, yet chose not to heal Lazarus. Lazarus was His friend, yet He had let Lazarus die when He had healed strangers. Why? She couldn't imagine why.

They reached the tomb, and Jesus stopped about twenty feet away. Mary and Martha came up beside Him, Mary's head buried in Martha's shoulder.

"Take away the stone," Jesus said.

"But, Lord," said Martha, "by this time, he stinks, for he has been dead for four days." Jesus looked at Martha.

"Did I not tell you that if you believe, you will see the glory of God?"

Glory of God Mary thought. How is my brother's death a glory to God?

Martha motioned for the four closest of the mourners behind her to roll away the stone, and they rushed to do her bidding.

At first, the four struggled to even budge the boulder, but finally, after a long, heavy push, it rolled just a little. After the first few inches, the momentum and weight of the giant rock allowed them to more easily move it the next few feet until the stone hit a small boulder near the cave. The four didn't even try to move the rock anymore as they had accomplished the goal. The tomb entrance was uncovered.

The four had been concentrating on moving the stone so much that they hadn't noticed the stench of decay until they had finished rolling it and took in a deep breath. They immediately regretted it as their noses were assaulted with the foul, palpable stench of decaying bodies. They covered their mouths and ran back into the crowd gagging.

Mary smelled the foul stench, as well, but it was not strong enough to cause any significant discomfort.

Jesus looked up into heaven and prayed, "Father, I thank you that you have heard me. I know that you always hear me, but I say this for the benefit of the people standing here, that they may believe that you sent me."

When He had said this, He called in a loud voice, "Lazarus, come out!"

Mary looked up from her sister's shoulder, hope filling the emptiness in her heart as Jesus spoke. She stared at the entrance, knowing her younger brother would walk through the threshold any moment.

Long seconds passed, and she stared, filled with hope. Lazarus had not come out. More long seconds passed, and still, she did not see her brother. Doubt crept in. She was so sure Lazarus would step through the entrance to the tomb, but he didn't.

Jesus had never failed before, and she knew Him to be powerful. More long seconds passed and still no Lazarus. Maybe Jesus couldn't bring him back. Perhaps death was stronger than Him.

It had been only a minute, but it was the longest minute of Mary's life. Jesus had spoken, but nothing had come to pass.

She felt a pit in her stomach; her brother was truly dead. It wasn't fair. Her heart felt like it had sunk to her feet. She felt even worse than before when she knew her brother was dead. Now, Jesus had given her hope, and that hope was being ripped from her.

She heard a chuckle from one of the "mourners," but she didn't care. She stared at the entrance to the cave. Despite knowing her brother would never walk through, she stared. It was hopeless. Her faith in her dear friend was forever altered. She would never look on Jesus the same way, she knew.

More long seconds passed, and more snickers emerged from the crowd of "mourners." Mary was on the verge of leaving Jesus and her sister. Nothing could change her brother's fate now, not even Jesus.

The snickers grew into pockets of chuckling and whispered mocking.

Mary looked at Jesus, knowing that He could hear the chuckling and mocking. He ignored them and merely looked toward the tomb entrance in expectancy.

She took one last look toward the cave entrance before she allowed herself to fall into a deep, dark cavern of despair and walk away from Jesus forever.

She saw a shadow move in the darkness of the cave.

She froze.

Her heart skipped a beat.

Her pulse quickened.

Hope flooded back from the abyss she had sent it.

The crowd fell silent as they too saw the shadowy form.

It hopped, seemed to fall against the wall, then hopped again.

The shadowy form, closer to the entrance now, had the form of a person but with no arms. It looked as though it had only one massive leg.

Then, it hopped again, emerging into the low light of the cave entrance. It fell forward, not having a wall to lean on, revealing itself fully to the crowd.

The crowd gasped as they realized who it was. It was Lazarus. He was still wrapped in his grave clothes. His arms were tightly wrapped in front of his chest in an "x" and his legs were wrapped together so tightly that he couldn't even shuffle his feet. He had to hop, and he could barely do that.

Mary's heart filled with elation. She had never been so joyous in her life. She stood there, still frozen, tears streaming down her face, so incredibly grateful and happy that her brother was alive.

"Take off the grave clothes and let him go," Jesus ordered.

Jesus' words drew her from her trance of elation, and she was the first to reach her brother with Martha right behind her.

Lazarus' two sisters unwrapped his face as he lay on the warm dirt and kissed his face over and over in joy. Their brother had come back to life.

It took the two of them several minutes to fully release their brother from his bonds as they continued to stop unwrapping him to hug and kiss him, they were so happy.

Jesus stood with the crowd, which soon began to praise Jesus for His miracle. He ignored them and watched

His best friends in their joy. All three had the grandest of smiles on their faces.

It wasn't long before the crowd left, leaving only Mary, Martha, Lazarus, Jesus, and the disciples. The three siblings, now genuinely understanding the glory of Jesus, transitioned into worshipping Jesus.

Though the disciples were used to this by now, it made them each uncomfortable at the zeal of the three siblings. The disciples eventually moved further away from the four until Jesus had finally informed the family that He had to leave.

The three begged Jesus and the disciples to stay, but Jesus insisted that He must continue about His Father's business and informed them that He would soon return. The three siblings followed Jesus and the disciples to the edge of the town, Mary and Martha wrapping an arm around their brother. They said their goodbyes, eternally grateful, and watched the thirteen men vanish into the distance.

Legion

Legion sat in the small cave he thought of as home. He was completely naked with scars that ran along his body. Some were years old. Others were fresh, with a few having been inflicted even as recently as a few days ago. He was unkempt, dirty. His long curly hair was matted with dirt and spider webs. He was covered head to toe in dirt, and his teeth were rotting. His long black beard showed signs of gray, but it was almost imperceptible amongst the bugs and grime coating it. He snatched a bug from his beard and ate it, hearing the crunching as its warm innards squirted into his mouth. As he chewed, the crunching echoed through his ears amongst the many voices. He looked about his cave, thinking – or, more accurately, hearing. Hearing the voices in his head. He could never keep a coherent thought for too long, and for the majority of his day, he really couldn't speak coherently

19

either. The voices in his head made it hard for him to understand anyone or to keep on a single train of thought. They were always screaming. They were always loud. He could never differentiate between what the legion of voices in his head were saying and what other people were saying. He could no longer tell which thoughts were his own thoughts and which thoughts had been planted in him by the voices. Thoughts of harm, hurt, pain, anger, despair, and more. Thoughts of cutting himself, even now as he sat there eating the bug. He didn't know if the thoughts of cutting himself were his or one of the legion of voices in his head, so he started scraping at his arms. He did this often, cutting himself with sharp rocks. He screamed in pain, but his urge to cut surpassed his pain and he cut more.

The urge subsided, and he darted out of his little cave, howling. The shackles around his ankles and wrists chaffing as they rubbed his skin raw, but he barely felt them now. They had been a part of him for years now, ever since the townspeople had bound him. He had broken the chains easily and scared the townspeople away. They left him to his own destructive ways now, out here away from everybody.

He howled and screamed, foaming at the mouth. The voices wanted him to scream and howl, to cut himself more. He screamed and howled, then saw the boat. There were thirteen men on board. For just a moment, he was clear-headed, the voices all distracted by the boat of thirteen men. He remembered what he used to be like, then, in that moment of calm, quiet, peace, clarity. Then, as quick as the calm in his mind came, it erupted in a flurry of voices, louder than he had ever had. Legion screamed, grabbed a nearby rock and started cutting himself again. He screamed louder from the pain. Hate and pain were filling his voice as they filled his mind. He ran, screaming and foaming at the mouth. He ran straight for the thirteen men getting off the boat. Fear and dread coursed through him now as he neared these men, his eyes focusing solely on just one of the thirteen, and he barely noticed the other twelve. Hate flooded through him in waves he had never felt. Fury so powerful it made him cry. He cried tears of pure outrage, and he wanted nothing more than to kill this man, to rip him limb from limb, but he knew he could not. That angered him even more. With tears of hate and rage, he cut at himself fueling his torment. His despair deepening his desire for self-mutilation, he cut at his face as he ran toward this man.

His thoughts – or thoughts of the legion, he couldn't tell, gripped him with fear, yet propelled him farther.

Finally, the man reached the group of thirteen, and they noticed him now. The man he hated stepped forward.

"What do you want with me, Jesus, Son of the Most High God?" Legion began as he fell to the ground, bowing, his voice trembling. "I beg you don't torture me!" This man, legion knew as Jesus looked down at him for a moment.

"What is your name?"

The man looked up erupting into a scream that seemed to echo as he cut himself with a rock from chest to stomach.

"My name is Legion! Ahhhhh! For we are many! Please don't send us away!"

"Legion," Jesus began. Legion howled and threw himself on his back. Jesus paused, staring at this demon-possessed man, His face stern and unrelenting. Legion thrashed about, throwing his arms and legs wildly, and tossing his head back and forth, screaming as loud as he could. He stopped suddenly as he saw a herd of pigs in the distance, near a cliff. He climbed back to his knees, bowing low.

"Please, allow us to go into the pigs! Please!" he begged.

"Very well, Legion, leave this man and enter the pigs."
With that, the man fell to his back, and with one last, long
howl, he arched his back. Then he was silent.

The pigs suddenly started squealing and panicking,
running straight off of the cliff.

Eldad lay on the ground, pain in every inch of him.
At first, he didn't realize he was naked. When he did, he
didn't care.

Everything was calm. Everything was quiet. He
was at peace. He looked at the sky, realizing its beauty in a
way he had never before noticed. He saw the faces of the
thirteen men who stood before him. He saw Jesus' face
and knew He was his deliverer. Though he hadn't any
clear memories of the past years, he sensed it was Him.

Eldad began to weep. "Thank you, oh, thank you,"
he said as he crawled back to his hands and knees and

began kissing Jesus's feet. "Thank you, oh, thank you," he wept.

One of the other men with Jesus bent low and draped a cloak over his naked body. He ignored it. He didn't care that he was naked. All he knew was that this man – this savior – had freed him from his demons.

***

Jesus, his disciples, and Eldad all sat on a group of small boulders talking. They didn't know how long they had been talking, but it had been some time. Eldad kept having sporadic episodes of overwhelming joy, resulting in him weeping from happiness and again thanking Jesus over and over. After his joyous episodes of thankfulness, the fourteen renewed their conversations that spanned anywhere from small talk to Jesus' teaching.

Several townspeople neared, slowing their pace as they noticed the man once called Legion. They murmured one to another.

"We are told you were the cause of our swine running off the cliff," one of the men said, his eyes periodically glancing at Eldad.

"He is!" Eldad spoke up, jumping from his seat on the rock. The townsmen stepped back, the leader raising a palm for Eldad to stay where he was.

Eldad stopped suddenly, understanding that they were afraid.

"We mean you no disrespect. We see that you are a great man of power." He pointed to Eldad. "We see what you can do. If you please, leave us at once, for your power upsets the lives of those who dwell here. We beg of you not to enter our cities, for we cannot have you upsetting our ways."

"Very well, we will leave at once," Jesus replied.

"Thank you, stranger."

Jesus nodded and turned to get in the boat.

"Master, Jesus, let me come and follow You. It is the least I could do for all You have done for me."

Jesus turned around as he sat in the boat, His disciples filing in after Him.

"No," He said. "Go home to your own people and tell them how much the Lord has done for you and how He has had mercy on you."

Eldad was conflicted. He was disappointed that Jesus had denied him the honor of following Him, learning from Him, and serving Him. Most of all, from walking with Him. However, he was given a task to serve his new-found Lord. He could walk with Jesus in a way by obeying His commission.

The man nodded, and with an excited wave goodbye, Eldad raced away. His one goal – to tell all who would listen what the Lord had done for him.

Renegade Christian

The king's army stood in formation, hundreds deep and hundreds wide, their armor gleaming in the bright sun. Off to the side stood a lone man, several feet from the formation. He didn't wear the standard army armor, but instead, he was lightly clad in studded leather.

"Hey," the lone warrior heard one of the soldiers on the edge of the formation whisper to the man next to him. "What's with that guy?" he asked.

The soldier next to him didn't have to look over to know what his friend meant.

"He's some kind of ranger. His name is Christian, I think. They call him 'The Renegade, Christian.' He doesn't fight with the army; he's more of a lone fighter. That's why he's standing way over there," the soldier explained.

"Why won't he fight alongside of us?"

"Nobody knows, really. Some think he has a death wish. Others claim he is too prideful to allow anyone to help him."

"Well, he better fight alongside this time; otherwise, he's going to end up dead real quick."

Christian looked over to the two soldiers in formation, and they both went silent, knowing that he had heard every word.

Christian didn't really care if they talked about him, but he was always amused whenever he looked toward those who were whispering or gossiping about him because they always stopped their conversations short when he did.

He didn't know what it was about him that intimidated people. On the battlefield, there was no equal, yes, but that was the battlefield. He very seldom spoke and that, he knew, made people uncomfortable. He could only assume it was a combination of his battle prowess and that he seldom engaged in conversation that made him so intimidating. That and the scar across his right eye and cheek.

He had never liked fighting alongside anyone. They Just seemed to slow him down or get in his way. His skill in battle was simply too far above anyone else's skill for them to keep up with him. He had decided long ago that he fought better alone. Solo.

The battle cry sounded, bringing him out of his thoughts. The army roared and charged onto the battlefield, Christian doing the same, alone, away from his comrades in arms.

Christian unslung his bow and nocked an arrow as he neared the first of many foes he would dispatch.

Arrow after arrow hit its mark without fail, and whenever he passed by a fallen enemy not dead, he finished him off with a dagger he had on his belt. With one swift motion he would kneel, unsheathe his dagger, and plunge it into his victim; then, he would roll, snatching up his arrow from the dying soldier as he sheathed his blade, never missing a step. Rolling to his feet, he'd fire the reused arrow and move on to the next victim, shooting another bolt or two into his nearest foe.

If the enemy soldier was already dead from the arrow, he merely yanked it out of the corpse and fired it at his next kill.

Target after target fell, arrow after arrow nocked and fired, he moved farther and farther away from his army.

Alone, he fought and killed dozens of enemy soldiers, none even nearing him due to his marksmanship with the bow. On the occasion an enemy did come within arm's length, he dispatched them quickly with his dagger and returned to firing arrows.

He saw a giant of a soldier then, barreling toward him. He stood a head taller than any soldier Christian had ever seen and he was twice the size of any man he had ever seen, with bulging muscles and armor that seemed too small for this giant.

Christian nocked an arrow and fired, hitting his target square in the chest. The arrow sunk deep into the breastplate armor. To Christian's surprise, the giant didn't waver; he didn't even seem to notice the arrow protruding from his chest.

Christian fired again. Again, the arrow hit its mark, and again, the giant of a man ignored it. He shot two more. The massive enemy soldier still came barreling toward him. He fired one last arrow, hitting the giant in the shoulder. The soldier still came; this time, he let out a bellowing scream. To Christian, it sounded more like anger than pain. Without a skip in his step, the giant yanked the arrow from his shoulder and swung his forearm across his chest, breaking off the arrow shafts protruding from his chest.

The giant was almost upon him now. He had spent too much time trying to down him with his arrows.

Christian dove to the side as the massive man brought his sword down. The sword dug deep into the soft ground, giving Christian just enough time to roll to his feet and unsheathe his dagger before the giant pulled his massive blade out of the soft ground and brought it around for another swing.

Christian easily dodged the swing with a duck as he sunk his dagger into the giant's calf, twisting the blade so the wound would not close.

The giant retaliated with a scream and hard kick. Christian, not fast enough to dodge the full force of the kick, caught the tip of the giant's boot in the ribs and heard a crack. Pain erupted through his side as he tumbled to the ground. His mind raced now, with confusion and fear, doubt and panic. How could anyone not be affected by five arrows? How can a wounded leg kick with that much power? For the first time in battle, he doubted his ability to defeat his foe.

He could only imagine if the enemy soldier had managed to kick him with full force. He didn't want to think about it.

The enemy soldier charged at Christian again, his sword raised for a fatal blow. Christian scrambled to his feet, pain surging through his side with every minuscule movement, and with all of his might, dove into the path of this massive enemy. His side erupted in excruciating pain as he contacted with this giant. He landed a shoulder right on his attacker's elbow, burying his dagger into the inside of his enemy's elbow in the process.

The impact jarred Christian to the core, though he barely noticed as his mind exploded in a cloud of pain from his side.

He fell to the ground, dropping his dagger and clutching his side. The enemy soldier lost his grip on his massive sword and it too thudded to the ground. The impact from Christian's charge sent him stumbling backward a mere single step.

He regained his balance, and again, charged Christian.

Christian still lay on the ground, oblivious to anything but the pain in his side. It wasn't until he felt the massive hands clutching him by his studded armor that he even noticed the gigantic man before him.

The enemy soldier lifted him with an angry scream, blood dripping down his arm where he had been stabbed, rage fueling his scream. He lifted Christian over his head, and with a howl of anger, he threw him as hard as he could to the ground.

New waves of pain surged through Christian's body as his enemy lifted him. With every tiny movement of

Christian's body, voluntary or involuntary, pain flooded his side.

He slammed, hard, into the ground, knocking the breath from his lungs. The excruciating pain from his side sent waves of dizziness through his mind and blackness threatened to overtake him. He couldn't breathe. He felt only pain, and saw his foe raising a hand for another strike. Then, just as darkness came, he saw a blurry form smash into his deadly enemy. All went black.

He woke to the angry scream of the giant. Pain surged through his side, and a broken shield lay beside him. He could tell from the insignia of an eagle that it was a shield of a fellow man at arms. He slowly stood to his feet, looking toward the sound of his enemy's screams. Surrounding the giant stood four soldiers. Two of them he recognized as the two soldiers whispering about him in formation.

One by one, his counterparts were knocked to the ground. Christian had never seen a foe as powerful as this man. Even with all of his injuries, he was stronger than three men. The soldier would charge toward the fallen soldier only to be attacked by the other three, keeping him from annihilating their fallen comrade.

The giant would quickly send another to the ground with a powerful kick or hit, but before he could finish him off, the last two attacked with even more fierceness than before. Again, the enemy soldier would down another only to be countered by the recovered ally soldiers.

Christian recognized the strategy almost immediately and saw several openings that would suit his arrows well. He found his bow and several arrows a few feet away and nocked an arrow. He breathed through the surges of pain in his side as he pulled back on the string, then waited for an opening. The second he had a clear shot, he fired. The arrow hit its mark, right in the neck of the giant soldier. He stumbled sideways as the arrow

penetrated his thick skin. This gave the other soldiers an

opening, as well. Christian nocked another arrow; breathing

through the pain, he pulled back on his bowstring, firing as

the opportunity presented itself. Another true shot to the

neck and the soldier finally dropped to his knees. Seconds

later, he fell dead as the four soldiers in combat took

advantage of their openings.

The four soldiers all turned and nodded before

turning back around and searching out another enemy.

The two who Christian had recognized lingered just

a few seconds longer, allowing Christian to nod a silent

thank you.

Christian himself fought on, as well, however

adjusting his tactics. He ventured back into the frays of

battle more cautious: first, because of his injury, and

second, because he began to understand that in combat,

though one might be a great warrior, there will always

come a time when winning the battle will depend on how well one fights alongside others because not all battles can be won alone.

Christian followed the two soldiers he knew responsible for saving his life and fired arrow after arrow, defending them in battle. The three dispatched more enemy soldiers that day than any other fellow men at arms and saved each other's lives a dozen times over.

Christian knew one thing now; he would no longer fight alone. He had his brothers to fight alongside, now. He would no longer be 'The Renegade, Christian.'

Naaman

Naaman stood at the edge of the Jordan River, staring at the flowing, brown, murky water. Why must he wash in this filth? He thought angrily. He was better than this, an honored war hero, respected among even his enemies, rich, powerful; yet, here he was—at the Jordan about to jump in. What was he thinking? Why would he want to plunge into that filth? He could go back home and live a fine life, not the life that he hoped he would have after today, but it wasn't a bad life.

He looked at his hands then—a reminder of why he was standing here. A reminder of who he was. His hands were scarred, but not by battle wounds. In fact, he had few battle wounds. He was scarred with disease. His hands were rough with bumps. Most were simple bumps that were unsightly. However, others were black, and others were yellow and continuously oozed pus. The latter were

40

the fewest, but they seemed to concentrate at his chest and back. There were even a few on his face. He always had a cloth with him to wipe the seeping bumps on his face. When supplies allowed, he bandaged the unsightly, pus-filled boils. This was why he was standing here, to be rid of this leprosy.

He took a deep breath and stripped off his clothes and, with a scowl on his face, jumped in.

The water was cold, sending a shiver through him, and he could immediately feel the grime in the water. It felt like he was standing in a river mixed with charcoal. He lifted his hands and rubbed the tips of his fingers together. He could feel the grime scraping at his fingertips.

He slapped the water repeatedly, violently, splashing muddy water in all directions and immediately regretted it as he accidentally splashed some in his mouth, tasting the revolting dirt and began frantically spitting, trying to rid himself of the foul taste.

He slapped the water angrily one last time, took a deep breath, and dunked himself into the water.

Again, he felt the charcoal-like grime scrape across his now submerged chest and backside as the Jordan's water flowed. He could almost feel the muck sticking to him, refusing to release itself from his diseased face and body. He wasn't sure if it really was piling on his face as the water rushed past him or if it was in his imagination, but one thing he knew for sure was that he was better than this filth.

He stood back up, bringing his upper body back out of the dirty water, and looked at his hands.

***

Naaman walked among his men encamped at what they called "the pass." It was early evening, and the sun had set, reducing the temperature, as well as the visibility, and the men at the camp had quickly set up fires.

Naaman always kept a cloak on, even when it was hot. One reason for this was that it kept the direct sunlight off of him, which seemed to keep him just a little cooler, and he kept it on in the evening for warmth. He was also acutely aware of how unsightly he was, so he covered as much of himself as possible. He always kept his hood low so that its shadow concealed his face—as well as a shadow could.

He wound his way through the camp, nodding his hooded head in acknowledgment when his soldiers stood as he passed. They huddled in groups of six or eight around their fires, sharpening their swords and eating dinner. Their tents were spread out near the fires on both sides to help break the wind.

Naaman could see the tension in their faces, even in the seasoned soldiers who tried not to show it. This was expected, however—it is always expected the night before a battle. The army mentally prepared itself for combat.

The men readied themselves for death and accepted the fact

that they may lose their friends the following day. They all

knew that many would not live past tomorrow, and they all

secretly hoped it wouldn't be them.

Naaman felt the same, despite his skill with the

sword and his veteran status. Mortality always brought

with it a heaviness—no matter who you were. He made his

rounds and settled into his own commander's tent to

prepare himself for battle—and death.

***

There had been no change. He still had the

unsightly leprosy. This had only been his first dip;

however, he couldn't help but feel frustration with this

entire situation. Why did the prophet tell him to dip seven

times and not just once? All he wanted to do at this

moment was to get out of this filthy water. Why did the

prophet not just heal him on the spot, instead of making

44

him do *this*? He realized his anger had subsided, though, and he was merely frustrated now rather than infuriated.

He could still feel the grime, and it seemed to him that the grime was beginning to pile on him now, thickening. This could, of course, only be all in his mind, he knew. He took a deep breath and fell backward, this time, splashing into the water, again feeling a new wave of grime scrape across his upper body as it plummeted into the filth of the Jordan.

***

Naaman stood near the back of the battle lines, as was his ritual before battle. He could see the enemy in formation and saw them in their last moments of preparation before they attacked.

He trotted his horse through the formation, which opened a path like a wave, receding, then closing back in as he passed. He noticed, as he guided his horse through the line, several of his soldier's faces as he passed by—newer

soldiers under his command. They had not yet gotten used
to his presence—the presence of a leper—and he could see
the fear on their faces. Fear of getting too close as they
took a couple of extra steps away, pushing against their
fellow soldiers in the formation, their eyes wide with fear.

Naaman didn't let this bother him, and he brushed it
off, though he felt a prick to his heart as it only reminded
him of who he was—what he was. As honored as he was,
he was still an outcast, of sorts.

When he reached the front line, he dismounted his
horse and patted its hindquarters. It neighed and galloped
down the line of soldiers. The soldiers, having fought
many battles under his command, readied their weapons as
they knew this to be the sign that the battle was about to be
underway.

Naaman watched the horse until it reached the end
of the formation then turned to face his enemy. He dropped
his cloak, revealing only cloth leggings and standard

soldiers' footwear. He had no shirt, no helmet, no armor, merely his sword in hand and not even a scabbard.

His men cheered, their unified voices a resounding roar.

Naaman sprinted toward the enemy formation, his army mere steps behind him.

＊

Naaman raised himself back up from the grimy water of the Jordan. He could feel the grit of the river on him even more now, it seemed. He wondered if it was all in his head, or if it really was clinging to him. He despised having to stand in the midst of this muck, but he knew that if he truly wanted to be healed that he needed to be here—despite his strong preferences to the contrary.

He slowly lifted his hands out of the water, his heart beating in anticipation. Still no change, and he dipped himself again.

＊

Naaman, having been in the throes of battle for several minutes and feeling the excitement and exhilaration of combat, charged his next opponent, who saw him mere seconds before Naaman was upon him. The enemy soldier had just downed one of Naaman's men and turned just in time to see Naaman charging him, mere feet away. The sight of Naaman's almost naked and grotesque form took him aback, and he hesitated, which cost him his life.

Naaman, of course, knew this as he saw the fear and horror in the enemy soldier's eyes as Naaman barreled down on him, sword cutting through the air toward its target. Naaman pulled his weapon from the dying man's stomach and, without missing a beat, brought his sword into the path of another enemy soldier. Naaman forced his enemy's sword down, the grinding of the two steel blades scraping against each other seemed only to spur him on. He stepped closer to his enemy, leaving himself open for an elbow or fist, yet none came.

Naaman knew why. Always in battle, when his heart was pumping fast, the sores oozed at an almost steady and constant pace. He could feel the pus running down his back and chest in small streaks. He could feel it pooling at his elbows when he bent them. It dripped from the sores on his face, and, on occasion, he tasted the warm, foul, sweet fluid as it touched the corner of his mouth. This only added to his intimidation. As he neared his opponents, he would blow and spit hard, projecting the pus out in all directions and making him look like a madman.

His newest opponent soon fell dead to the ground. Again, Naaman knew that just as much as it was his skill with the blade, it was also his appearance that won his battles. Deep inside, beyond the pride, beyond the power, beyond the fame, he felt embarrassment. He felt weak. He felt alone. He suppressed these emotions just as quickly as they rose and found his next victim.

***

Naaman stood back up in the water, its grimy and slimy contents of no concern to him now. He wasn't angry at having to dip himself in the Jordan anymore. He wasn't hopeful that he would be healed, either. He simply stood straight up. Something had snapped inside him as he dipped himself that last time. He remembered his last battle. A great victory and a great many emotions. He remembered how he felt during the fight. Those emotions he so often buried because there was no hope for him— now, there was hope, and yet, he felt nothing.

He looked at his hands almost robotically, fully expecting nothing different. They were still the same. Three times and nothing; what was there to suggest this fourth time would be any different?

He took a shallow breath and leaned back into the water slowly, until everything but his face was submerged. He dipped himself more on autopilot now. He still had three more after this one—then, he would see how true this prophet was and his God.

He allowed the waves of the Jordan to wash over his face then stood back up. A wave of emotion flooded him then and memories, memories of all that he couldn't have as a leper, his only torture—being himself. He fell forward, utterly and entirely alone—not only here at the river, but in life as a whole.

***

The enemy fled, their army decimated by two thirds, and rather than dying, they dropped their swords and ran. Naaman's army yelled in victory, each hugging the soldier next to them. Naaman stood there, his sores oozing and dripping down his face and bare chest and back. He could feel his pants were now soaked through with sweat and puss, sticking tightly to him. He slowly spun, looking into the eyes of those near him and nodding in victory. An overzealous celebrator who had just finished celebrating with his neighboring fellow soldier turned, his arms wide for a victory hug toward Naaman but stopped short as he realized it was his commander.

Naaman nodded in understanding with a smile, pretending it didn't bother him. In truth, that moment stabbed him deeper than any sword ever could. It reminded him, yet again, that he would never feel companionship as others did.

He looked around, noticing soldier after soldier clasping wrists or hugging in victory, yet he stood alone. Alone now, among thousands of battle-hardened warriors, none wanting to chance catching his leprosy by touching him—especially now.

He would never clasp wrists with a counterpart, would never hug a fellow soldier in victory—would never feel the warmth of a woman. His closest friends had never touched him, let alone his current wife—a marriage more of convenience and stature than anything else. He would forever be condemned to keep a solitary existence, never to touch another soul in any meaningful way.

***

Naaman re-emerged from the dirty water. It felt on his skin like he felt inside—dirty. Dirty like his oozing, disease-riddled skin. He looked at his hands almost out of habit now than anything else. They had not changed. He turned them palm up and saw now that they were wrinkly. He had been in the water not that long, yet they were already wrinkly—like his soul—a soul that felt old and tired of life. He had dipped himself five times now, and not one sore had even shrunk or stopped oozing. What if this didn't work? Could he live the rest of his life with no hope after feeling even just this tinge of hope he had today?

He was tempted just to climb out of the Jordan and go home, accepting that even the God of the Israelites couldn't, or wouldn't, heal him. Two more, he thought, might as well finish the seven and see if anything will actually happen.

Naaman fought through his doubting and, this time, dove back down into the water, fearing that he would give up if he allowed himself to fall slowly into this river.

***

Naaman walked among his men, most of whom were drinking in victory, some mourning the passing of their counterparts in battle, and others attending to their injured brethren, or injured themselves. The soldiers, as they noticed him pass by, stood in honor and recognition of him. He nodded back, and they returned to whatever it was that they were doing. The injured or those tending to the injured ignored him, not out of spite, but simply because if those tending to the wounded stopped, it may have negative consequences, and those who were injured might injure themselves even worse. Naaman knew that they meant no disrespect.

He noticed a severely injured soldier near the outskirts of the encampment, his leg cut clean off, the attendants constantly tending to him. They had cauterized the wound so it had stopped bleeding; however, the injury was still grave. The attendants kept constant watch over him and his wound, keeping the bandages as clean as possible, the wound free from the wind that carried dirt, and gave him a numbing tonic often to help with the pain.

Naaman walked over to the injured man and his attendants.

"How is he?" Naaman asked.

"He is in pain, as expected, but it is too early to tell if he will survive," the attendant answered.

"I see," Naaman replied as he bent low to take a closer look at the man's half leg. He noticed something on the bandages and instinctively reached out for it. The man shifted his leg away as Naaman reached out. Naaman paused, then, his hands a few inches from the wound. He looked down and noticed yellow puss dripping off of the knuckle of one of his hands. He looked up at the injured soldier, realizing the fear that must have been racing through the man's heart.

Naaman was about to touch this man's bandages with oozing sores. He was about to touch the man's wounded stub. A stub that still seeped blood, though not enough to cause him loss.

Naaman pulled his hands back and hid them under his cloak, wiping the puss from his knuckles only to feel more puss accumulating on them again.

He smiled at the man, noticing the dread in his eyes.

"You will be fine," he said to the man missing half of his leg. He turned to the attendants and nodded, then left.

Naaman left the confines of the camp, walking into the night desert until the fires from the camp no longer hindered his vision. He stood in the dark, lit only by the moonlight. He looked up at the moon and stars, then pulled his oozing hands out from his cloak. He watched the pus accumulate on his knuckles, then drip down to the desert ground. He watched it pooling on the desert floor, too thick to be absorbed by the dirt. Then he saw an insect crawl over to it, not hesitating to run headlong into the pus. It sat in the pool of discharge not moving. The thick pus sitting there with this bug.

Naaman thought then, men feared him, women were revolted by him, and insects were drawn to him. With everything he had, his fame, his power, his wealth, he would give it all up for just one touch from a woman, one kiss from a loved one, one caring clasp of the wrist from a fellow swordsman, one victory hug after a battle. He would never get those things, no matter how much he wanted them.

He lifted his foot and brought it down on the bug. The crack of the insect's exoskeleton resounded in his ears.

The crushing of the bug, a symbol for the crushing of his dreams of ever having a real family the day that he noticed the first of the sores. Like his flesh, his soul was filled with sores that oozed with hopelessness, though he kept his feelings secret and shoved them down within him and locked them up as best he could, they inevitably resurfaced—more than he liked.

He turned and walked back to the camp, the cold night a reflection of his soul.

***

Naaman leaped up from the water, taking in a deep breath. He had allowed himself to stay under too long. His thoughts raced through his mind as the waters raced across his face under the water. With his breath flooded in his emotions. He knew he hadn't yet been healed; he didn't need to look at his hands to know this, but he did anyway. As he knew, he had not been healed. Six times now he had done as he was told. Six times nothing, absolutely nothing, had happened. What if, on this last time, still nothing happened? What if this was all a complete waste of time? What if the God of the Israelites did not heal him?

He decided, then, that if this God did not heal him, that he would dip himself an eighth time and never raise back up. He would kill himself. He couldn't live like this anymore. No contact with another person. Constantly wiping himself of this disgusting ooze. Always having to purchase new clothes after only a few weeks as his sores ruined them.

He refused to live anymore if this God would not heal him. He would not allow himself to live. If he couldn't have the willpower to keep himself under water until he died, then he would run off the nearby cliff. At least then, all the willpower he would need to muster would be that one last step.

The last dip—the seventh dip—felt like the longest dip as his mind raced with all of the possible outcomes. It was when his doubt was the strongest, yet it was when his faith was the strongest. He had already decided what he would do if the Israelite God would not heal him, but he had not decided what he would do if the Israelite God did heal him.

He feared to raise himself back up, yet he feared to stay under the oppression of these sores. He closed his eyes and slowly lifted himself up. He stood tall, despite his fear. He had not felt anything, just like the other six times. He lifted his hands in front of his face, his eyes still closed. Fear gripped him. He did not want to die, but he couldn't live as a leper any longer. Not now, not after the hope he had been given, false as it might turn out to be—hope is hope, whether it is false or not.

He held his hands up to his face, closing his eyes tightly. He stood like that for mere seconds, but, to him, they felt like hours. He slowly lifted his eyelids, opening his eyes. Everything was blurry; he had held his eyes so tightly shut that they had to adjust to the light again. Again, it was only seconds, but those seconds seemed like hours.

His eyes cleared and almost immediately blurred again as he saw his hands. They were completely smooth. He gasped in shock and excitement. His heart raced, and his eyes watered with tears of joy. He looked down at his chest. It was completely smooth. Not a single sore. He looked at his arms, again, clear of disease. He whimpered. Not a whimper of fear or sorrow, but a whimper of joy. He touched his face, feeling his skin. His face was smooth. Smoother than he knew it should have been. He noticed that his face felt soft, gentle, wrinkle-free. He knew he should have wrinkles, but he did not. He felt his chest again and realized the same. A completely smooth chest. His skin felt like it should be that of a twenty-year-old or a young boy's skin. He rubbed his arms, then wrapped his arms across his back, feeling the smoothness of his back.

He gasped again, noticing that even his battle scars were gone! He had not realized that until he had felt where the worst of his scars should have been. His back. He looked and touched his chest again, where he knew should have been scars. Then he wept. He cried, and his knees weakened. He waded his way to the river's bank, holding himself up until he could compose himself enough to climb out.

When he finally did climb out, he realized that he now had a new problem. He had not thought to bring any fresh clothes, and he didn't want to put on his old, dirty, tainted clothing. He was completely new, and completely naked, and didn't want to chance getting infected with leprosy again—especially not from his own pus-filled clothes and not so soon after gaining this new body.

He left the river bank naked, enjoying everything, and concerned for nothing.

The Valley of Dry Bones

The prophet of The Most High God walked among countless bones. He had been spirited away from his home by God just minutes before.

He was careful not to step on any of the bones. It was a task with every step that he took as he took not one normal step. He stepped to the left, between the legs of one skeleton, then crossed his other foot farther to the left, finding the only space not claimed by the remnants of a fallen soldier, between the pelvis of the same skeleton and head of another. He took a long stride to the right, between the legs of another skeleton, and another short left step next between a decapitated skull and its counterpart skeleton.

He continued this zig-zag approach to keep from desecrating any of the skeletal remains of this massive army. Though his God had not told him not to break any of the fragile, dry, sun-bleached bones, he felt a sense that this place had a holy purpose, and they should not be disturbed.

His God had transported him there by the spirit and had told him to walk among the bones in the valley. The valley he knew to be a valley where a great battle was fought, the bones before him, as far as the eye could see in all directions—or at least until the edge of the valley walls—lay thousands and thousands of bones.

Some were half engulfed by earth. Skeletons buried as if the ground itself stopped short of devouring them. A skull screaming for salvation as mounds of dirt protruded from its eye sockets and bulged from its open mouth as if the earth was in the process of swallowing a screaming man. Half-buried arms and legs stretched out from the ground as if reaching out, hoping someone would take hold of them and drag them to safety far from the maw of the great earth devouring them.

Others the vengeful earth seemed to spare, leaving the entirety of the skeleton frozen in time in the positions of their deaths. Untouched by earth, they stared out amongst their counterparts, waiting.

He heard his God then, again. A booming voice that seemed to come from everywhere. A voice that demanded obedience, filled with absolute power. A voice that struck fear in his heart and tinged with a softness that brought with it peace. It always baffled Ezekiel, no matter how many times his God spoke to him, how He could evoke such terror, yet such peace, in his heart simultaneously, how his God could evoke such contradicting emotions at the same time.

"Man," the booming voice of God said. "Can these bones live?"

Ezekiel knew that they were dead; yet, he also knew his God was indeed all-powerful and so knew if God wanted them to live, they would live.

"Lord, God," he replied at last, "only you know."

"Prophesy to these bones and say to them, 'Dry bones, hear the word of the LORD. This is what the Lord GOD says to the bones: I will cause breath to enter you, so you will come to life. I will put muscles on you and flesh on you and cover you with skin. Then, I will put breath in you so you will come to life. Then you will know I am the LORD'."

Without hesitation, Ezekiel began to prophesy as he was commanded.

"Dry bones, hear the word of the LORD . . ." The ground began to rattle, and a loud noise erupted in the valley. Ezekiel, startled, paused in his prophesying and stumbled back a step as the rattling grew to a full shaking of the ground. "This is . . ." he continued through a shaking voice. "What the Lord GOD says to the bones: . . ." The noise grew louder and louder as he spoke these few words, and the ground shook violently. "I will cause breath to enter you so you will come to life . . ." The noise and shaking reached its pinnacle, and it took Ezekiel his all not to cower and run; he stood his ground, fear gripping him, the ground beneath him shaking so violently that he struggled to stay upright, shifting his feet back and forth, barely catching his balance with every step and every shake of the earth.

What he saw next brought a new wave of awe and terror into his heart. The bones before him slid from their resting places, shaking just as violently as the ground before him. They connected bone to bone, each piece finding its counterparts without error.

Most bones moved mere inches, the skeletons having not been touched by time or animal. Some, however, found their counterpart several feet or even yards away as they were dismembered or scattered, either by the passage of time or the ferocity of the battle itself. Skulls slid into the necks of their corresponding bodies and shattered arms, legs, and midsections reintegrated themselves and slid into whole skeletons.

The most terrifying, however, was the half-buried skeletons or pieces as they shook themselves free of their earthen prisons. The earth shed itself out of the skulls' eyes and mouths, sending clumps of dirt and plumes of dust into the air. The half-buried arms seemed to grab air with a crack as the dried, crusted earth encasing them broke into pieces, sending clumps of dirt and plumes of dust into the air, as well. The midsections and legs of the skeletons also shot clumps of dirt and plumes of dust as they too broke free of their prisons. The once partially buried skeletons slid their fragmented selves together, only partially visible from the haze of dust surrounding them.

Within seconds, the bones had all come together to form rows of fully formed skeletal remains. The dust already being carried away by the faint breeze.

Ezekiel took a deep breath, mustering all the courage within himself and continued to prophesy. The ground had stopped shaking, and the noise had ceased, yet what he saw next as he continued sent chills of awe and amazement through him at the power of his God.

"I will put muscles on you . . ." His voice trailed off as he watched the scene unfold before him, and with every breath, he had to concentrate on his next words as he saw the bodies form right before his very eyes.

"And . . . flesh . . . on . . . you . . ." he said slowly, watching. "And . . . cover . . . you . . . with . . . skin."

As he spoke the first of those words, the ground seemed to seep blood. The blood gathered on the bones as more blood seeped up from the ground gathering near the bones. The blood began to solidify on the ground into dark red slabs of meat with slivers of white Ezekiel soon recognized as muscle. The newly formed slabs of muscle rolled along the ground, rolling onto the bloody skeletons, grabbing tightly to the bones as more blood seeped up from the ground. The blood streamed onto the muscles, soaking into the muscle slabs. Muscle sinews grew from the muscle slabs strangling each other, grafting themselves into their neighboring muscles.

As he began prophesying the growth of the flesh, he saw that the muscles started to grow and thicken from blood-soaked, sinewy, red, mushiness into a layer of brown, tanned, porous skin.

"Then, I will put breath in you, so you will come to life. Then, you will know that I am the LORD," he finished.

Ezekiel was relieved that he finally finished his prophesy as he saw the final pieces of it unfold. The lifeless bodies grew hair, eyes, nails, and the skin pigments changed to varying shades of brown.

He stood still, his worn brown robes and long hair waving in the wind. He was expecting the bodies now to stand up, as everything else that he prophesied had

happened as he spoke, but nothing else happened. He stood

waiting for his God to finish His work. Still, nothing

happened.

"Prophesy to the wind," came the booming voice of

his God. "Prophesy, man, and say to the wind, 'This is

what the Lord God says: Wind come from the four winds

and breathe on these people who were killed so they can

come back to life.'"

Ezekiel immediately did as commanded. As he

repeated the words the Lord, his God, told him to say, the

valley suddenly erupted into a great wind. Not an east

wind or a west wind, but a wind that came from all

directions. It was a fierce wind, and it took Ezekiel his all

to keep from being blown over. He planted his feet,

bracing himself against the wind as it pushed and pulled at

him from every direction. His brown robes flapped hard in

the winds wildly. They slapped at him, and they pulled at

him to release them from the confinement around him. They fought him with every second, slapping and pulling, as if they had become a sentient being struggling against their captor.

The wind, in seconds, grew so loud and strong that he had to finish his prophecy yelling with all his breath over the screaming wind.

Ezekiel noticed as he spoke the prophecy and the wind assaulted him that the wind did not affect the lifeless bodies lying before him. Dust engulfed the valley floor knee-high, swirling as if it were a foggy mist, then billowing out as if attacking an unknown foe above it and, finally, falling back onto the lifeless bodies that still seemed untouched by the violent wind threatening to knock Ezekiel to the ground.

The dust, just for an instant, fell heavily on the bodies, allowing Ezekiel a flash of the bodies before swirling back up into a foggy mist again and continuing the cycle again and again.

The few seconds it took Ezekiel to finish the prophecy through the powerful and awe-inspiring winds he glimpsed, with each of the three times the dust cleared for just a moment, it seemed some item of clothing formed around the naked bodies in the valley, as if the earth itself were forming and wrapping them in new clothes.

As Ezekiel finished the prophecy, the winds died, and the dust cleared. Scores of lifeless bodies lie before him, fully clothed in leather armor.

The lack of wind now made the valley seem too quiet to Ezekiel, and he waited for another miracle from his God—as if what he had seen as of yet was not astonishing enough.

Suddenly, all in unison, the dead came to life, sitting up in shock with a sudden and deep gasp of air. It startled Ezekiel, and he took a couple steps back, kicking a foot behind him, which made him lurch forward as he spun, seeing whom he accidentally kicked, almost kicking another foot as he recovered. The man ignored him.

The vast army of newly revived men each stood to their feet, looking at their limbs or touching a neighbor, the shock of their resurrection and new life still fresh.

Ezekiel knew the last thing they probably remembered was their deaths.

Ezekiel's God spoke, then, the deep billowing voice that seemed to come from everywhere. As the vast army realized what being it was that spoke, they fell to the valley floor with their heads bowed as low as they could dip them.

The voice of God explained to Ezekiel that the valley of dried bones was a representation of His own people and that He would bring them out of their graves, putting His spirit in them, bringing them to life, and putting them in their own land.

Then the Lord, his God, fell silent, and Ezekiel and
the great resurrected army marveled at what God had done
that day.

<u>Bonus Short Stories</u>

Dee & Dean, Quest of a Coward

The two neared the edge of the continent. They had been running for hours. They knew it was only a matter of time before someone discovered that they had crossed the boundary.

"Dean! Let's go!" yelled the first of the two to reach the edge.

"I Don't know, Dee. Maybe this wasn't a good idea," Dean replied, slowing as he neared the edge.

They were both abnormally tall, over six feet tall. Both wore the white robes of a high priest, and both looked remarkably similar. Though they had only met months ago, by their appearance, one might think them siblings.

Dean had short raven black hair and dark eyes, while Dee had short blonde hair and light gray eyes.

Dee rushed back to Dean. "We have to do this. Remember, that's why you asked me to help you, because you knew you couldn't do this yourself." He took Dean by the shoulders. "Now, come on. I'll be with you every step of the way."

Dean nodded. "O-okay," he replied, fear exuding from him like a cloud. Dee released him and reached into his satchel.

"Now reach into your bag and think about the harpoon gun you put in there yesterday. It'll come to you. We don't have a lot of time, they have probably figured out that we aren't in the temple and are probably on their way to stop us," explained Dee.

"Okay," Dean said nervously.

"Now come on," Dee said as he turned and walked back to the edge of the continent.

He looked out into the vast horizon of fog, as Dean came up beside him. "It is beautiful, isn't it?" Dee commented. Dean did not say a word, he merely stared off into the distance in complete terror.

All they could see, except one small island several hundred yards away, was white fog. They could barely see the island through the fog, and it seemed as if it were something out of a dream. The island did not look solid, the white fog all around it.

Dee reached into his satchel and pulled out his harpoon gun. The harpoon was a massive thing. Without the magical properties of their satchels, they would be loaded down with supplies, making their journey that much more difficult and slow. Thankfully, though, the satchels would accommodate objects of any size or weight. The bags never grew any larger or heavier, regardless of how much gear was packed into them.

Dean saw Dee take his harpoon out and did the same. "You ready, Dean?" Dee asked.

"Yeah," Dean answered in a whisper.

"Okay, let's do this." Dee fired the harpoon into the fog toward the island. The steel rod shot out with a whoosh, followed by the hissing of the rope attached to the spear as it slid out from the satchel. A few seconds later, the rope stopped. Dee pulled on the rope, testing its secureness, then nodded to Dean. Dean fired his harpoon gun, and seconds later his rope stopped. He checked the rope as Dee had done.

"Dee, what happens if my spear comes out?"

"It won't Dean. Even if it does, I'm here to get you. You won't get far before I get you." Dean nodded, not entirely satisfied with the answer.

"If you're that concerned, reach in your satchel and grab the end of the rope. Tie it around your waist and then to me." Dean immediately did so, not noticing Dee's look of irritation at his cowardice.

"You ready, now?" Dee asked as he tied the end of Dee's rope around his own waist. Dean nodded. "Good, follow me." Dee took a running jump off of the continent into the unknown oblivion of whiteness.

Dee didn't fall, as he knew he wouldn't, but floated out straight in the direction he had jumped. Gravity was of little consequence out past the floating land masses. There was still gravity, but it did not have the same effect as it did on the land masses.

He spun himself around to see Dean still standing at the edge of the continent. Frustrated, he took Dean's rope tied around his waist and yanked as hard as he could. He laughed as he saw Dean fall off of the edge and slowly float toward him.

Dean was suddenly yanked from the safety of the edge of the landmass and into the terrifying fog of nothingness. He flailed about, reaching for the edge of the floating continent. He frantically stretched for the ground, but it was too late. He was already out of reach. Fear gripped him as he saw the giant land mass floating before him, he was too scared to admire the awesomeness of the giant rock. It seemed to go for miles in depth, he could actually see where the soft dirt on the surface of the continent changed to hard rock. He looked down to the bottom but couldn't see it. The land mass curved like a bowl and was far too big for him to ever see the bottom - unless he fell down.

Something pulled at him again, and he turned around to see Dee yanking on his rope again. He floated faster toward Dee now, and just moments later he was beside him.

"Alright, Dean. Let's make our way to the island." Dee said and pulled on his own rope, moving away from Dean.

Dean frantically grabbed for his own rope attached to the spear he shot and pulled until it became taut, then yanked hard, propelling himself toward the island.

A few minutes later, they both floated onto the surface of the small island.

"Now, that wasn't so bad, was it?" Dee asked.

Dean shook his head, "No."

"As long as you know what you're doing, you'll be just fine." Dean nodded in understanding.

"Okay." Dee said.

"Okay, let's keep going. They aren't far behind us," Dee said.

Dean nodded.

"Now reset your harpoon. We are going to do the same thing to get to the next island." Dee pointed to the other side of the tiny land mass they stood on. Past the fog they could see another similar island, but it was much larger. The one they stood on was not more than twenty yards long, tiny compared to the next one.

"We have three more islands to go. Then we'll be there," Dee explained as he re-loaded his harpoon gun, pulling another spear from his satchel. Dee looked up to see Dean slowly re-loading robotically. Then, Dean just stood there.

Dee untied the rope from the bolt embedded in a nearby tree. "Check your rope around your waist. Make sure it's tight. I'll check mine in a minute. We don't want to get separated when we are jumping. You know, just in case."

Dean did as he was told, looking up in panic when Dee mentioned getting separated.

Dee saw his sudden fear and took Dean by the shoulders. "It's only a precaution. Kind of like the second harpoon you have in your satchel. It's not like we're going to need it, but we just want to be safe rather than sorry, okay."

Dean nodded.

"Okay, now after you check your lifeline, untie the rope from your harpoon in the tree and fasten it on your new spear. Make sure it's tight."

Dean nodded again, and Dee released his shoulders, motioning for him to get the rope from the bolt.

They successfully made the jump to the next island. Dee told Dean to untie himself and put everything back into his satchel. "It'll be a three-day hike across this island according to the map," Dee explained. "We will hike until dark, then set camp."

Two days later, Dean and Dee sat by a small campfire. They were quiet, too tired for conversation. Dean sat watching Dee as he stared into the fire, roasting a small rodent he caught.

Fear kept its choking grasp on him but loosened just a bit when Dean thought of his friend Dee. Dee was everything he wanted to be. He was brave, smart, quick thinking, confident, and never seemed to be caught off guard.

He didn't know why, but at times like this, when things were less scary, Dean felt sad as he looked at Dee. Not because Dee was better than him in every way, but some other reason. Dean couldn't say precisely why he was sad for Dee, but sometimes it felt as if Dee was not really there, or that Dee would be gone soon. He could not make sense of it. He did not know what it meant, but Dee had been by his side since that fateful day when everything had changed only six months ago.

"You're burning your food," Dee informed, bringing Dean from his thoughts.

Dean had been cooking his own rodent in the fire, and as he lost himself in thought had unintentionally lowered the meal deep into the heart of the flames, charring it.

"Oh!" Dean exclaimed as he saw his food on fire. He quickly pulled it out of the fire and blew out the flames clinging to the dead animal.

The two ate their meals in silence and soon retired for the night.

By nightfall on the third day, they had reached the edge of the island and waited until dawn the next morning to harpoon to the next piece of land.

They had noticed that the fog had shifted from white to a pink tint. It would have concerned Dean a great deal before this journey began, but he had become slightly less fearful over the past few days. Though fear lurked within every corner of his mind, he was better able to suppress it. He attributed this to having Dee beside him during these frightful times, making things less scary for him.

In fact, jumping to the next island was remarkably easier for Dean than the first two jumps, and he didn't wait for the prodding of Dee before jumping.

The next two islands were quite a distance away and could not be seen through the thick fog, but the harpoons and the map ensured their success in reaching the next few islands without a problem. This, too, would have been of great concern to Dee when first beginning this journey, but he followed Dee, trusting, now, that Dee would not let him down.

It seemed that the fog deepened several shades of red with both islands they harpooned to, and the fog looked eerily sinister now.

"We are here," Dee said as they reached the edge of the third island. "That," he pointed to an evil looking island surrounded in deep, dark, red fog, "is our destination." The island was barren, with only dead weeds and trees.

Dean stared in horror at the island, fear choking him once again. He could barely swallow as he stared at that menacing island. Even the red fog seemed to swirl angrily around it.

"Are you ready for this?" Dee asked.

Dean nodded.

"Well let's go, then." Dee shot his harpoon, then jumped off the edge.

Dee robotically shot his own harpoon and with a deep breath, closed his eyes, stepping off of the edge.

He pulled himself closer to the menacing island. With every pull, his fear grew, his throat tightened, and his muscles became more rigid.

Finally, he stepped onto the dead, lifeless island and turned to Dee. Dee stood there smiling. "You did it, Dean, you did it," he congratulated.

Dean stared at Dee, not knowing why, but knowing something was wrong.

"Congratulations friend, you did it," Dee said with a large grin on his face as he began stepping backward. "You don't need me anymore. Goodbye, dear friend." Dee started to vanish. He did not fade into the dark, red fog, but vanished into nothingness. "Stay brave," Dee said as he disappeared, his voice trailing off and echoing into the depths of the decay of the island.

Dean stood in shock, not fully understanding what had transpired, but remembering, suddenly who Dee was. Remembering that Dee was dead. He had been dead six months. Dee was dead because of him. He had killed his only, his best friend. He dropped to his knees sobbing. It was because of his cowardice that Dee was dead. If only he had been more courageous before. If only he had fought past the fear, Dee would still be alive.

Dean was not sure if all of this was in his mind or if Dee had actually been there with him those six months, and he could not explain why he did not recognize Dee before now. Something had gone terribly wrong six months ago, and it was Dean's fault.

Dean knew one thing for sure, though.

He felt release.

Rite of Ascension

Ohano stood with his father, looking out into the wilderness.

"Today is a meaningful day, Ohano," his father said. "You will begin your rite of ascension into manhood today."

Ohano stood still, staring out into the dry desert, sparse with small brush. Fear gripped him like he had never felt before, and he held so tightly to the spear his father had given him for the quest that his knuckles turned white.

"You will find the kind of man you will be," his father continued, resting a hand on Ohano's shoulder. "It is a three-day walk to the Tinleaf grove. You each must return with your leaf. Do you understand?" His father waited for Ohano to answer, gently squeezing Ohano's shoulder when he did not reply.

"Ohano, do you understand your quest?" Ohano slowly looked up at his father and began to cry.

"I don't want to go," he said. Ohano's father knelt down so that he stood eye to eye with his son.

"You must, Ohano. It is the way of our people. You will never be respected, and you will never become a real man if you do not." Ohano cried even more.

"Don't make me go, Father. I don't want to become a man." Ohano's father stood.

"You will go," he said firmly, "and you will stay gone eight days, no less. You will return with the Tinleaf." Ohano heard the finality in his father's voice. It was harsh, unsympathetic, and demanding.

Ohano's tears flowed now. His father's features softened at the sight of his son crying so freely.

"You cry now, a boy, but you will return a man without tears," he said and pushed his son away from him. "Go," he ordered, his tone calloused.

Ohano wiped the tears from his eyes and stared at his father. "I'm scared," Ohano whispered through a shaken voice. "I can't." Ohano's father pointed toward the wilderness, his face stern.

Ohano turned, noticing the other boy's fathers doing the same. They had each had similar conversations and had all been forced to partake of this rite of ascension. They were all turning thirteen, the age when a boy begins becoming a man. To become a real man, one had to retrieve the Tinleaf, so they were sent on a quest to become men, and this quest would tell them what kind of men they would become.

The three other boys made their way to him, wiping tears from their eyes. They didn't say anything, but Ohano knew they were looking to him for direction. He wiped away his tears and slowly turned toward the wilderness. He took a deep breath and started walking.

He tried to recount what his father had told him about the journey. The first day, they would be walking in the mildly dry desert they lived in now with little shade. Depending on how quickly they walked, they would reach the rock lands within a few hours to half a day on their second day. There, they would have to be wary of the wolves. The land shortly after that would begin to get lush and green. When this happened, they would be close to the small forest that held the Tinleaf grove.

They walked for hours, not speaking a word. Eventually, they stopped crying. The sun was setting, and their stomachs began to growl.

"I'm hungry," complained Matono.

"Me too," added Towano.

Matono and Towano were cousins and looked remarkably similar, so much so that they could be mistaken for brothers. The other boy, Enyetu, was taller and scrawnier than the rest of them, and his complexion was several shades lighter than the dark brown skin of the other boys. He agreed with Matono and Towano.

Ohano stopped, looking at the other boys. "So am I. We will need to hunt."

"Hunt? By ourselves?" asked Enyetu. "We have never hunted by ourselves."

Ohano nodded. "I know, but we have with our fathers."

This seemed to convince the others to try to hunt, and so they hunted for hours, searching for rodents that might have a nest, but found little in the sparsely vegetated wilderness. Then, they gave up on hunting animals and searched for reptiles. They could not catch any and gave up this shortly after, as well.

They went to bed that night with growling stomachs. They didn't sleep well either because they weren't allowed to take anything with them except a single spear, and all they wore were animal skin loin coverings.

They shivered most of the night, used to the hot sun and animal skin blankets at night.

They were able to start a fire, but it didn't help much with the cold as the wind blew out what small fire they could start.

Ohano was the first to wake the next morning, partly because he heard the skittering of a lizard as it wandered by. He scrambled to his feet as fast as he could and dove for the little creature. It darted away, but not before Ohano caught its tail between his fingers.

Ohano's sudden attacking of the lizard awoke the others with a shriek.

"I almost had it!" Ohano hollered upon noticing that they had woken up.

"Look! Look!" He held up the lizard tail, still between his fingers. The boys scowled at him for waking them up in such a frightening fashion and stretched then tried unsuccessfully to catch breakfast.

Though he still couldn't catch breakfast, Ohano's experience with almost catching the lizard gave him the confidence for the rest of the day to keep trying to catch or spear any creature he saw as he led the boys toward the Tinleaf.

Every so often, he would hold up a hand, as he had seen his father do on hunting trips, and then throw his spear. The other boys would similarly ready their spears as well in hopes of finally finding food.

Near noonday, the four reached the rocky terrain and, as the wildlife seemed to grow in number, Ohano finally caught a lizard. Soon after, one of the other boys speared a rabbit rummaging near underbrush, and they started a fire to cook their freshly caught meals. Things seemed to be going well for them now as they had finally caught food and started the fire rather easily.

They were all briefed by their fathers on the dangers in this part of their journey, and so, as they continued their journey and began traveling through the rocky terrain, they stayed alert. They walked in single file with their spears up, ready to throw or defend themselves. They walked as quietly as they could and jumped at every loose pebble falling, lizard scurrying, or unfamiliar noise.

They noticed, as they were told they would, their surroundings getting lusher as they traveled the sparse, rocky terrain as it began morphing into dense, green, heavy underbrush with soft grass. The rocks eventually gave way to smooth ground, as well, and soon, the four could see the forest.

They decided to set camp just inside the edge of the small forest where the trees would block the wind, and they could keep a fire burning. They had agreed to take turns on watch as they were taught when hunting.

The next morning, they easily caught breakfast and followed the directions given by their fathers to walk about half a day's journey to the center of the forest where they would find the Tinleaf grove.

They saw the grove easily, a patch of huge, deep purple leaves about the size of their heads. They each pulled a leaf off the large green and purple vine and staked the thick, furry, massive leaves onto their spears, pulling them down about halfway.

"We are men now," said Towano.

"Not yet," Ohano replied. "We still have to go home."

The first half of their journey home seemed much easier and swifter than their trip to the grove. They constantly joked and commented about being real men and the kind of men they would be.

They had become confident in their abilities to hunt, travel, and kill by themselves, and they were less alert on their return journey.

On their second day of traveling home, they were almost through the dangerous, rocky terrain when a blurry form jumped from the cover of a nearby rock, tackling Ohano.

The three boys saw Ohano tumble to the ground in a heap of fur and skin, a fright-filled scream filling the air.

They barely saw the two additional wolves in time as they charged and dove for the next two boys, Towano and Matono. Now alert, though caught off-guard, they did see the wolves in time to bring their spears up. Matono wasn't quick enough, and he and his attacker tumbled to the ground, the vicious beast growling and snapping as Matono desperately defended himself.

Towano was able to bring his spear up in time and skewered the wolf as it lunged at him; both tumbled to the ground, the wolf yelping as it fell dead.

Enyetu sprang into action, seeing Matono entangled in deadly combat. He jabbed his spear into the wolf. It too let out a dying yelp.

Luck was with Ohano as the wolf lunged at him. He had been using his spear as a walking stick, which saved his life. The spear caught between Ohano and the wolf kept the wolf from taking a bite out of Ohano's jugular. They tumbled to the ground.

Still holding the spear, Ohano rolled, trying to fling the heavy creature off of him, but he was not strong enough to lift the animal.

Somehow, the animal shifted its weight, and Ohano saw the creature's deadly teeth closing in for a fatal attack. He did the only thing he could think to do and shoved his forearm into the creature's path. The teeth sank deep into Ohano's arm, and he let out a pain-felt scream feeling the vicious animal's teeth scraping bone.

He struggled against the wolf's powerful maw as he slid his other hand close to the tip of his spear, maneuvering it so the tip pointed toward the neck of the wolf. With all his might, he pushed forward with the arm the wolf had in its mouth and rolled.

Another surge of searing, cutting, stinging pain erupted across Ohano's chest, and the last thing he remembered was screaming.

He woke to such unbearable pain that he could barely speak.

He felt burning across his chest and on his arm. After a few moments, the shock wore off, and he lifted his burning arm to see purple mush compacted in the bite wounds. He instantly knew what it was, Tinleaf. It had medicinal value and would help to heal his wounds. He gently felt along the burning across his chest with his finger and looked down. His chest was sliced from his left shoulder down to his right hip. Blood had dried around the wound, and Tinleaf had been turned to mush and compacted in the wound, as well.

He looked up to his three friends who each wore a wolf pelt draped around a shoulder and had noticed him wake.

"Do not move," Matono ordered. "You have much healing to do."

"What did you do?" Ohano asked. "Why did you use the Tinleaf?"

"We could not let you die," Enyetu replied.

"Did you use all of it? We must go back and get more," Ohano said and sat up, only to scream out in pain and fall back down onto his back.

"We used three, yours is still on your spear," Towano said.

Ohano noticed Matono's wound, then.

"Why didn't you use mine on your wound?" Ohano asked.

"Mine is not that bad. Besides, you deserve to be a real man."

"No." Ohano shook his head. "You must use it, so you don't get sick."

"We all agreed, Ohano," Enyetu said. "You killed the wolf well. You fought with courage, and you were badly injured. You deserve to be a real man."

"No."

"It is settled; you will keep your Tinleaf." Towano said. "Now rest. When you are well enough, we will continue home."

Four days late, they neared their village. They had waited two full days for Ohano to get well enough to travel, and though the rest of their journey was without danger, they traveled slowly due to his injuries.

When the villagers saw them, they all ran to meet them, quickly noticing the wolf pelts, the injuries, and only one Tinleaf. The four could see the curious looks in their kinsmen's faces.

Ohano looked to the ground in shame, extending his spear. "We bring only one Tinleaf because of me," he said.

"Ohano is a real man; we are not," Matono added.

"Why did the four of you only bring back one Tinleaf?" asked the village elder.

"I was injured, and they used their Tinleaves to save me," Ohano said, ashamed. The elder looked to Ohano.

"And you did not offer your Tinleaf to help heal Matono?" he asked.

"He did," Matono answered, "but I would not let him."

"Why?" the elder asked.

"Because he fought bravely, like a real man and should become a real man," Matono said.

"And you all agree with Matono?" the elder asked.

Enyetu and Towano nodded.

"I see," the elder replied. "You have returned without Tinleaves. You all have done well."

The four looked up in astonishment at what the elder said.

"The true test of the rite of ascension is not the Tinleaf, but the journey in becoming the man you are during this quest. You all have honored your families and your tribe by your actions. Your actions have determined what kind of men you are. You are all real men."

The four boys—now men—looked at each other in glee and pride.

"You must all rest, especially you, Ohano. We look forward to learning what happened on your quest. You had us worried."

Ohano and the boys followed their kin back to the village. Ohano looked down at his cut filled with Tinleaf mush and gently ran his finger along the wound. It would scar, he knew. It would be a bad scar, an ugly scar. It would be a symbol of his manhood. How he became a real man. He smiled. He and his friends were real men now—all of them.

Hazards of the Office

Jim could see the commotion through the interior window, which served as a wall between his office and a large, multipurpose room they used for company-wide meetings or events. A dozen or so of his coworkers had congregated near an open window with more of his coworkers gathering nearby.

He dropped his pen on his desk and exited his office.

"Jim," whispered a nearby coworker, "there's someone out on the ledge."

"What! Who?" Jim asked.

"I don't know."

"Did someone call nine one one?"

"Yeah, I think so."

Jim saw the man on the ledge as he shimmied further away from the open window, sliding along the wall and onto another large window.

"Hey!" Jim said, "I know that guy." Jim rushed over to the open window, shoving his way through the crowd. He leaned out the window to get a better view of the man. It was who Jim had thought it to be.

He had met the man only once at an after-work birthday celebration for the boss. Jim had thought the guy weird when he met him. The man had isolated himself in a corner, eating his cake. Jim noticed he was by himself while everybody else was huddled in clusters conversating.

For the life of him, Jim couldn't remember the man's name, but he felt sorry for the guy. Jim could see the tears streaming down his face. Then, Jim did something dumb. He didn't know why he did it, and he didn't know what he was thinking, but he stepped out onto the ledge.

His heart raced, and his palms began sweating instantly. He regretted his decision almost immediately, but it was too late to turn back now.

He felt the wind blast him and he pressed himself into the wall, his heel slipping on the windowsill.

His heart leaped from his chest and his suit jacket suddenly felt like a lead weight. He recovered his footing quickly and inched his way toward the man, not wanting to slip on the windowsill again.

"What are you doing!" the man screamed. "Get back!" Jim barely registered the screaming as he was preoccupied with not dying.

He made the mistake of looking down the thirteen stories. Everything started spinning, and he felt like he was going to faint. He closed his eyes and pressed hard into the concrete wall.

"Leave me alone!" the man yelled.

Jim opened his eyes and slowly turned his head.

"Why did you come out here?!" the man asked.

Jim looked at him. "Honestly," he said, "I don't know. It was a stupid idea."

"Are you calling me stupid?!" the man screamed. "Well, I am stupid!"

"No, I'm calling me stupid, not you," Jim said.

The man stared at Jim.

"Besides, I'm guessing you actually have a reason to be out here," Jim continued.

The man still just stared.

"You're not stupid," Jim added.

"How do you know?" the man asked.

Jim noticed that the man's scream this time was a bit calmer. At least not as loud.

"You have no idea who I am or how dumb I am," the man continued.

"I know who you are."

"Yeah, what's my name?"

Jim noticed a tinge of hope in the man's voice.

Jim didn't know what to do. It was true that he didn't know the man's name.

"We met at Mr. Learney's birthday party, remember?" Jim replied.

The man looked disappointed.

"You don't know my name, do you?"

"No, I don't, but just because I don't know your name isn't a reason to kill yourself."

The man let out a guttural scoff and turned away from Jim.

Jim's heart raced. The man was about to jump.

"What is your name?" Jim asked. It was the only thing Jim could think to distract the man. The man turned back to Jim.

"You don't care," he said.

"I do. Look at me out here; I do care. What is your name?"

"Charles," he said.

"Charles? Charles is your name? Okay, well Charles, it's nice to meet you again."

Charles just stared.

"You will forgive me for not shaking your hand? I'm scared to death to move."

Charles nodded.

Jim noticed that Charles seemed a lot calmer now.

"Charles, let's go inside and talk."

"No!" Charles hollered.

"Why not?"

"Because I have nothing to live for."

"Yes, you do. Your life is something to live for." The moment the words escaped Jim's mouth, he knew how stupid it sounded.

Charles glared at him.

"You're right, that was stupid to say. Will you please tell me why you want to kill yourself?"

"It won't change anything."

"I know, but it will make me feel better."

Charles looked at him for a few long moments.

"My wife and my job," he said. "My wife left me last night, and I just got fired."

Jim, again, didn't know what to say. He wouldn't have known what to say in a normal situation, let alone standing on a ledge trying to save the guy from jumping.

"That is terrible news. I am very sorry to hear that," Jim said.

"Do you feel better?" Charles asked mockingly.

"No," Jim said instinctively.

Charles chuckled.

Jim's heart skipped a beat. Charles had found that funny. Maybe he was calming again. Jim still didn't know what to say, so he just started to say the first thing that came to his mind.

"I feel worse now, actually," he said.

"Why do you feel worse?" Charles asked.

Jim thought to himself that this was good. If he could keep Charles from thinking about himself, maybe he wouldn't jump.

"Well, to be honest, Charles, I'm thinking how stupid my problems are now."

"Like what?"

"Like what problems, you mean?"

Charles nodded.

"Well, let's see," Jim said. "I was thinking yesterday that I have a dentist appointment next week. I hate going to the dentist."

Charles chuckled again.

"I was thinking just a few minutes before coming out here with you that I wouldn't mind having a different job. Sitting here all day kind of stinks."

Charles smiled.

"You should try my job," Charles replied, then remembered that he no longer had the job. Jim saw the transformation on Charles' face and feared he would jump.

"Oh yeah, what was your job?" he asked.

Charles looked up.

"H.R.— I always had to deal with everybody's complaints about every little thing. Stupid things. My boss always gave me the stupid things like people complaining that the I.T. Department doesn't fix things fast enough."

"Ah, yeah. I would have jumped a long time ago," Jim joked then realized what he said. "Oh, God! I am sorry Charles, that wasn't funny."

Once Charles got over the shock of Jim's comment, he cracked a small smile.

"I probably should have jumped a long time ago."

"Charles," Jim's face grew serious. "Please don't jump," he said.

"Why not?"

"Because life is precious."

"Not mine," Charles replied as he looked down to the street, noticing the police lights and ambulance lights, as well as the crowds gathering.

"Yes, yours is, too. Listen, it might be bad right now, but things will get better. You will get another job, and your wife leaving really sucks, but the pain will go away."

Charles looked back at Jim.

"She cheated on me," he said.

"Listen, that really stinks, and that is despicable of her, but she isn't worth you killing yourself. Don't let her win."

Charles stared at Jim. Jim sensed he was getting through to him.

"What about all of the people that care about you? Friends, family?"

"I haven't talked to my dad in years, and my mom's dead. As for friends, I don't have any. Nobody likes me, everybody thinks I'm weird, and nobody will miss me."

Jim saw the despair creep back into Charles' countenance. He had just destroyed all of his progress with one question.

He didn't know what to say, so he just thought he should try honesty—brutal, harsh honesty.

"Okay, Charles, I am going to be honest with you, but promise me you won't jump."

Charles stared a few moments then nodded.

"You might not have people right now that care about you, but you *can* have people who care. You just have to be friendly and try to make friends. I'm not going to lie to you; you are weird, but don't let that be why you jump. You're weird, but right now, I want to get to know you. Let's see if a weird guy can be friends with me. Let's get off of here. I want to go home. I don't want to die out

118

here, falling off of this ledge. I don't want you to die either, even though I don't know you. Now let's go inside."

Charles stared at Jim, and for a moment, Jim thought he was going to jump.

"Okay," Charles said finally.

"Okay?" Jim replied.

"Okay, let's go inside," Charles said.

"Okay, let's go inside, then," Jim said.

Charles inched his way toward Jim, sliding against the window, then as he reached Jim, both inched their way back to the open window just a couple of feet away.

Jim slid himself along the concrete wall until he felt the window, then cautiously slid across the threshold of the windowsill. Charles did the same, carefully sliding across the first windowsill to the concrete then waited for Jim to crawl back through the open window.

Jim slowly bent low, slipping a leg inside the window and dangling it over the edge, the window too high for him to reach the floor. Then, his other foot slipped on the windowsill, and he fell backward.

He turned sideways, grabbing the window as he fell backward, but the weight of his body ripped him from his precious grasp on the window, and he fell. Grabbing the window allowed him to slow his fall and turn his body so his legs dangled off the ledge as he lost his grip. Half a dozen hands reached for him, but his arm slipped through their grasps. He clawed at the concrete ledge as his body pulled him over. Then, he felt a strong hand grab his wrist. He looked up to see Charles dangling half off the ledge, one hand inside the window and the other with a tight grasp on him.

"Pull!" he yelled up into the window as Jim reached up, grabbing Charles' hand with his free hand.

Charles was pulled to safety by three coworkers when another coworker grabbed Jim as he came within arm's reach and dragged Jim across the dangerous threshold to safety.

Charles and Jim stood to their feet, and the crowd cheered and patted Charles on the back. Several coworkers commented on how brave it was for Charles to rush to Jim's safety as he fell. Jim didn't know how Charles ended up laying on that window ledge, getting to him so fast without falling, but what mattered was that they were both okay. It seemed that all of his coworkers had forgotten why they were out on the ledge in the first place. It seemed that all they remembered was Charles rushing to Jim's aid on that ledge with no regard for his own life.

Jim smiled. He had saved Charles' life, and Charles had saved his life.

He would let Charles be the hero. Charles needed to be the hero.

If you liked the book, please leave a review on the store website that you bought the book.

Visit C. J. Korryn's website for more of his books.

http://authorcjkorryn.wixsite.com/officialwebsite/books

Connect with C. J. Korryn through:

Website:
http://authorcjkorryn.wixsite.com/officialwebsite/books

Blog:
https://authorcjkorryn.wixsite.com/blog

Twitter:
 https://twitter.com/cjkorryn

Facebook:
https://www.facebook.com/AUTHORCJKORRYN/

Instagram:
https://WWW.instagram.com/cjkorryn/

Printed in the USA
CPSIA information can be obtained
at www.ICGtesting.com
LVHW022010081223
765941LV00014B/1356